The SNOWMAN WALTZ

Written by Karen Konnerth

Illustrated by Emily Neilson

PUBLISHED BY SLEEPING BEAR PRESS

One, two, three,
One, two, three,
Here come the snowmen.

Swing, two, three,
Hop, two, three,
Gathering soon.

Bump, two, three,
Roll, two, three,
All through the winter.

Snowmen love waltzing out under the moon.

TEN-HUT!

One, two, three, four.
One, two, three, four.
Penguins marching in a line.

Left foot, right foot, turn together.
Yellow feet and beaks that shine.

Uniforms that all are matching.
Black and white and looking fine.

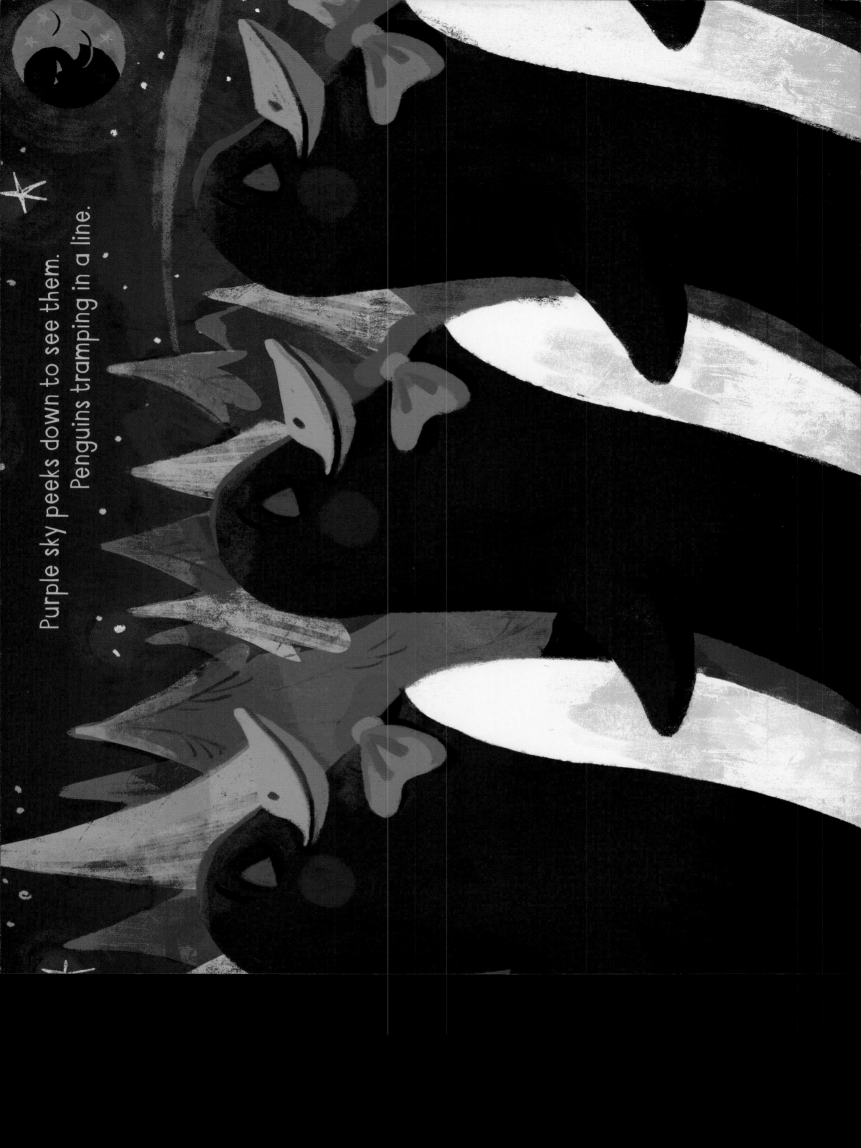

Purple sky peeks down to see them.
Penguins tramping in a line.

One, two, three,
One, two, three,
Over the river.

Spinning and laughing the faster they go.

There in the clearing the snowmen are dancing.

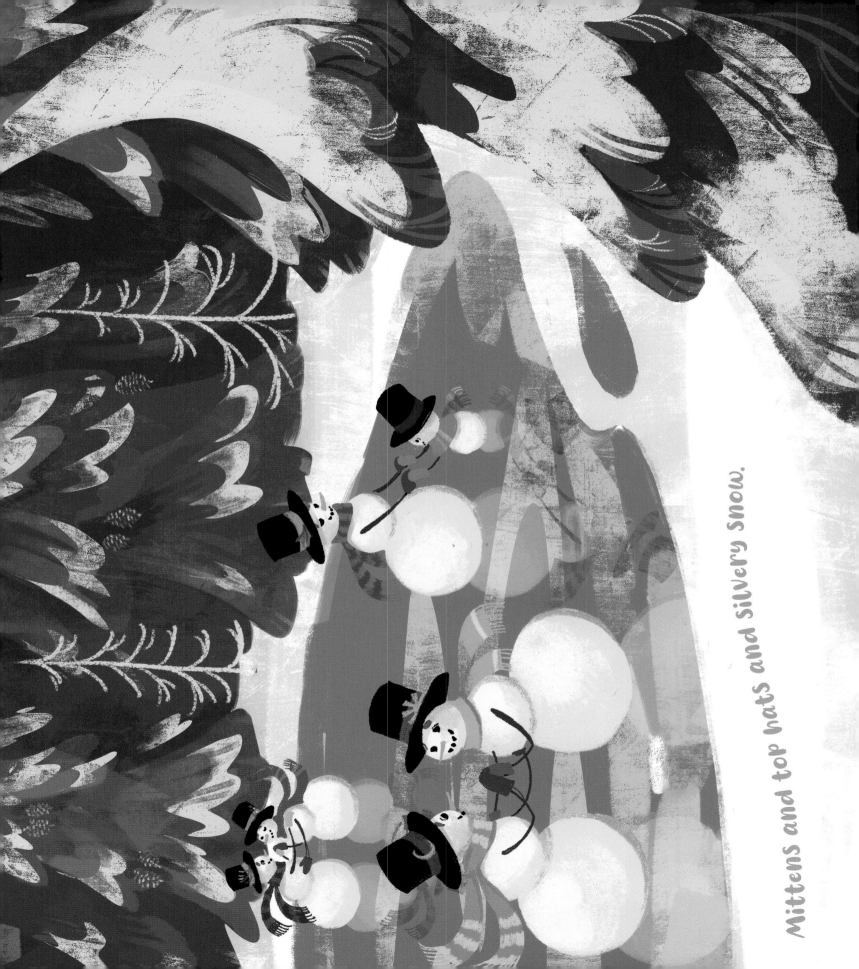

Mittens and top hats and silvery snow.

Step, two, three, four.
Step, two, three, four.

Penguins tramping big and small.

"Who is marching through our ball?"
Snowmen look and Snowmen wonder,

WHAT DISASTER! WHAT CONFUSION!

Penguins, snowmen shout and fall!

One, two, three,

One, two, three, four.

STOP! THIS DOESN'T WORK!

we WALTZ with a one, two, three!

Well, we MARCH with a one, two, three, four!

Hmmm.

Penguins line up oh so nicely,
Each a snowman by their side.

Marching, marching all together,
Penguins step and snowmen glide.

Back and forth they bump and waddle.
Having fun they slip and slide.

Then the snowmen show the penguins
Something that they never tried.

One, two, three,
Snowmen and penguins are waltzing.

Swing, two, three, stars sing a tune.
Glittering stars

Bump, two, three,
Slide, two, three,
All through the winter.

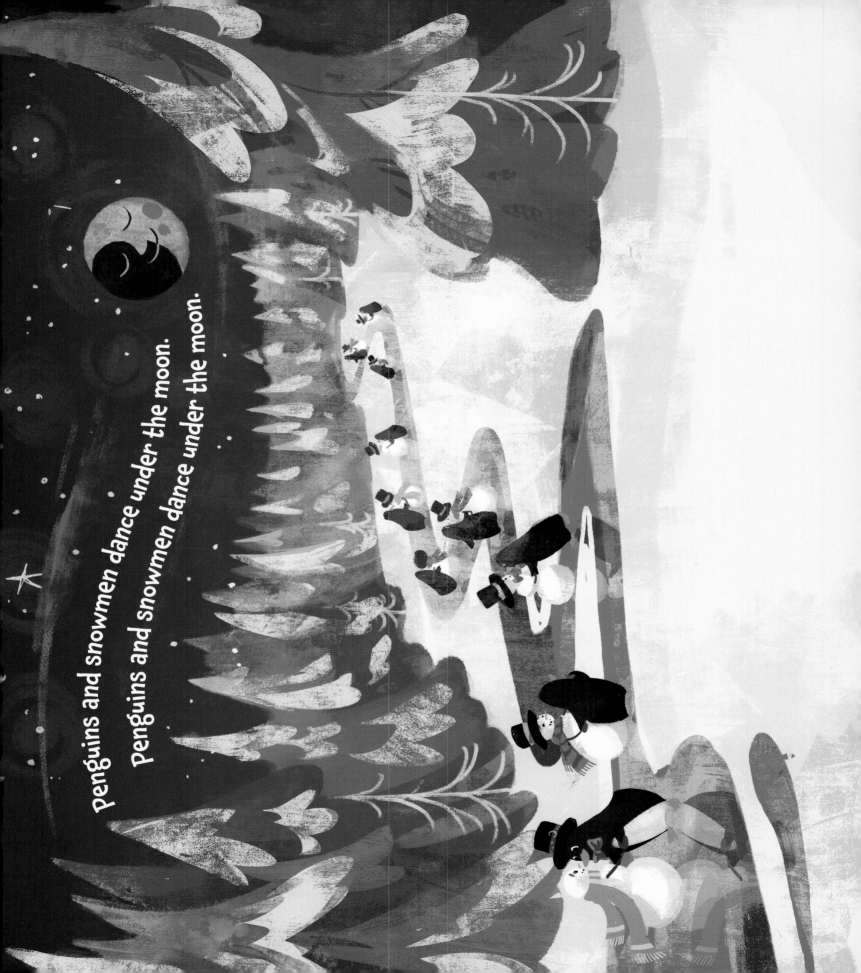

Penguins and snowmen dance under the moon.
Penguins and snowmen dance under the moon.

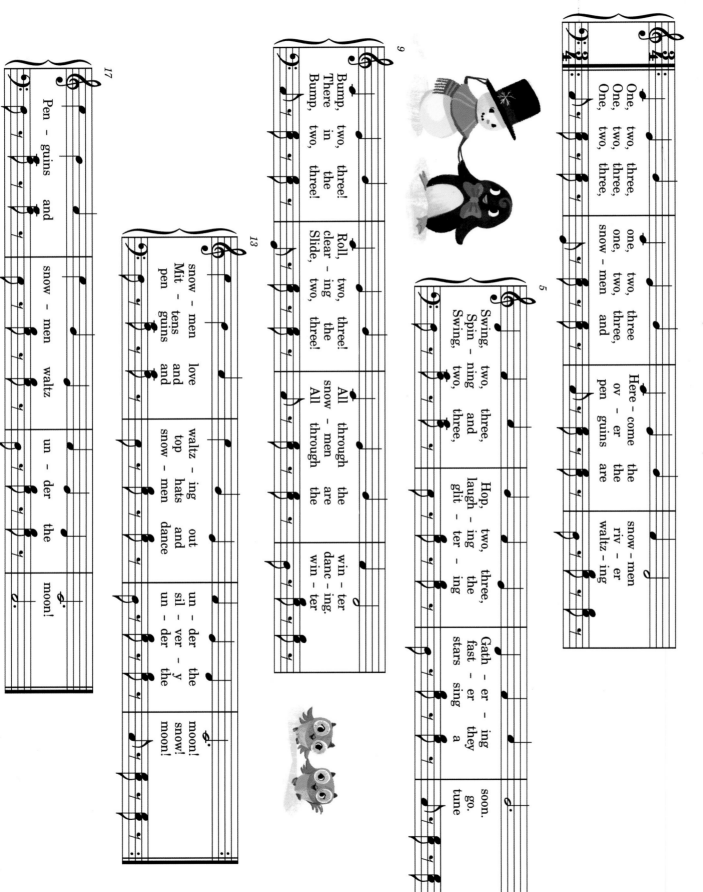

"THE SNOWMAN WALTZ"

Lyrics and music by Karen Konnerth

NOW YOU TRY!

Waltz with your fingers—then try with your feet!

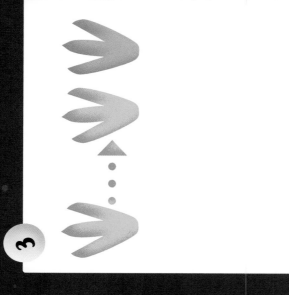

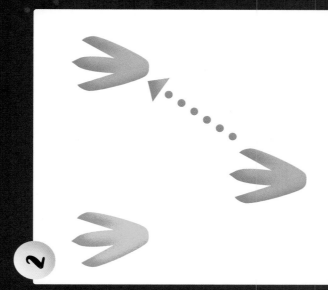

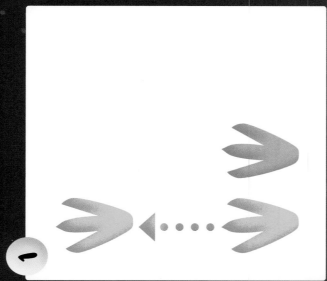

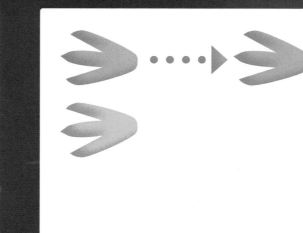

For Vic, my favorite waltz partner

—Karen

For G-ma and Omi

—Emily

SLEEPING BEAR PRESS™
2395 South Huron Parkway, Suite 200
Ann Arbor, MI 48104
www.sleepingbearpress.com

Printed and bound in the United States.

10 9 8 7 6 5 4 3 2 1

Library of Congress Cataloging-in-Publication Data

Names: Konnerth, Karen, author. | Neilson, Emily, illustrator.
Title: The snowman waltz / written by Karen Konnerth ; illustrated by Emily Neilson.
Description: Ann Arbor, MI : Sleeping Bear Press, [2022] | Audience: Ages 4-8. | Audience: Grades 2-3. | Summary: On a winter's night a dozen snowmen waltz in pairs along a frozen river to dance in a clearing, but they are interrupted by a dozen penguins, marching into the same direction.
Identifiers: LCCN 2022003608 | ISBN 9781534111271 (hardcover)
Subjects: CYAC: Stories in rhyme. | Dance—Fiction. | Snowmen—Fiction. | Penguins—Fiction. | LCGFT: Stories in rhyme. | Animal fiction. | Picture books.
Classification: LCC PZ8.3.K8414 Sn 2022 | DDC [Fic]—dc23
LC record available at https://lccn.loc.gov/2022003608